MAX LOVES MUÑECAS!

ZETTA ELLIOTT

MAX LOVES MUÑECAS!

ILLUSTRATED BY MAURICIO J. FLORES

Rosetta
Press

BOOKS BY ZETTA ELLIOTT

1

Max stood in front of the pastry shop. Behind the glass were rows of sugary tarts, luscious cupcakes, fruit pies, three-layer cakes, and ladyfingers dipped in chocolate. Max pressed his lips together and let his eyes roam past the delicious desserts. He wasn't hungry at all. What Max really wanted was to go next door.

Beside the pastry shop was a very special boutique. Inside were fancy, frothy dresses that looked like cotton candy, and beautiful handmade dolls. Every day, on their way

home from school, girls clustered around
the boutique's window, admiring the ever-
changing display. Max wanted to press his
face against the glass and admire the dresses,
too. But boys didn't like lace, and satin, and
tulle—did they?

Max knew he would be teased if he ever
admitted that he liked looking at dolls. He
didn't want to play with them *really*…he just
wanted to know how they were made. Each
doll in the boutique's window had a perfectly
painted face. Some had skin the color of
coffee; others had skin the color of cream.
Each doll had a unique dress trimmed with
pearls, or glass beads, or intricate lace. Some
of the dolls had coils of yarn piled atop their
head. Others wore carefully embroidered
caps that flipped up to reveal pierced ears!

"How do you make jewelry for dolls?" Max wondered. He wished there was a way to find out.

Max had never been inside the beautiful boutique. Sometimes he would stand behind the tight knot of tittering girls, shifting from foot to foot.

"Hey, Ava," Max would say casually. "What homework do we have for Math?"

Ava would groan and roll her eyes, but she always turned around, unzipped her bag, and took out her notebook.

"The homework was written on the board, Max," Ava would say.

Max would just grin and pretend to copy Ava's notes while taking a closer look at the boutique window.

Sometimes the other girls noticed that

Max was looking at the dresses and dolls. One or two times they laughed at him.

"Max loves muñecas!" they would chant until Max's face flushed with shame. Other times the girls didn't really seem to mind. They even told him which dresses they planned to wear when it was time for their quinceañera.

One day while Max was standing with the girls admiring the new window display, a bell tinkled softly and the door to the boutique opened wide.

"Bienvenidos!" said an elderly gentleman with warm brown eyes. "Welcome, everyone—come in!"

The girls rushed inside, each one pausing to say, "Buenos dias, Señor Pepe!"

The old man smiled at the girls and then

looked at Max. "Are you coming, m'ijo?"

Max pressed his lips together and quickly glanced up and down the block. What if someone saw him going into the doll shop?

Max could hear excited ooohs and aaahs as the girls discovered new and wonderful things. Max swallowed hard, nodded once, and slipped inside the boutique.

What a sight met his eyes! Carousel ponies pranced across the wall, glittering crystals dangled from the chandelier, and beautiful dolls were everywhere!

Max felt like he was dreaming. While the girls gushed over the gorgeous gowns, Max went from doll to doll, marveling at their beautiful bracelets, elegant earrings, and pretty pearl necklaces. Señor Pepe sat on a stool behind the counter and watched Max over his slender spectacles.

"Do you like dolls, m'ijo?" he asked finally.

Max felt his face grow hot. He nodded shyly and put his hands in his pockets, though he yearned to touch the soft, chenille hair cascading down one doll's back.

"You know," said Señor Pepe, "I once knew other boys who loved to work with dolls."

Max looked up, amazed. "Really?"

Señor Pepe nodded, but kept his eyes on the new dress he was making. Max drew closer and watched as the silver needle dipped in and out of the shimmering fabric.

"When I was a boy," Señor Pepe said, "there was no shame in making something beautiful with your hands. Sewing is a skill—

just like hitting a baseball or fixing a car."

Max had never thought of it that way. "How did *you* learn to sew?" he asked.

"Do you really want to know? It is a very long story," warned Señor Pepe.

Max set his heavy book bag down on the floor. "I don't mind," he replied.

Señor Pepe smiled but his eyes looked somewhat sad. "I learned from the best when I was a small boy. But that was long ago and far away."

Ava came over to the counter. "We're going now, Max," she said.

Max shifted from foot to foot. He glanced at Señor Pepe, but the old man was busy sewing. "I—I think I'm going to stay," Max said timidly.

Señor Pepe stood and reached for a

painted tin full of biscuits. He offered them to the girls as they filed out of the store. Then Señor Pepe returned to his stool behind the counter. "Pull up a chair and have a cookie," he told Max. That's when Señor Pepe's story began…

2.

Pepe lived in a one-room house with his grandmother. They were poor, but they loved one another very much. Every morning Pepe helped his grandmother clean the home of a wealthy family that lived up in the hills. Sometimes the señora gave them old clothes, towels, or sheets her family no longer needed. From these Pepe and his grandmother made new clothes for themselves, a beautiful patchwork quilt for their bed, and dozens of charming rag dolls.

In the afternoon Pepe and his

grandmother often went to the beach to sell their homemade dolls to the tourists. Sometimes Pepe was allowed to play with the other boys on the beach. Sometimes he was not.

"Always remember," Abuela would say, "you are not a street boy."

Pepe knew his grandmother did not approve of the boys who roamed the street, causing mischief and sometimes stealing from tourists or vendors in the market. But all the street boys were not like that. Pepe often saw other boys his age selling things they had made with their hands.

"Street boys are not so very different from me," Pepe thought to himself. But Abuela disagreed.

"You have a home to come back to, and

someone who loves you," she told Pepe. "You do not drift from place to place like a weed in the sea."

Sunday was Pepe's favorite day. After church Abuela took Pepe to the public garden. Hand in hand they strolled down the cobbled paths, breathing in the fragrant perfume of the beautiful flowers. Abuela could name them all: zinnias, ginger lilies, orchids, ixoras, hibiscus, bougainvillea, and plumbago.

As they walked home from the garden, the sea breeze washed over the boardwalk, leaving a soft, salty kiss on their cheeks. Pepe squeezed his grandmother's hand and felt like the luckiest boy in the world.

Then, one Sunday morning, Abuela did not wake up. Pepe slipped out of bed and started his chores. After he had swept the front yard, Pepe tried once more to wake his grandmother. Realizing something was wrong, Pepe ran next door to get help from a neighbor. Señora Clemencia came back with Pepe and told him his beloved grandmother had passed during the night.

After the funeral, all the ladies in black went away. Pepe sat on the bed he had shared with his grandmother, unsure what to do.

"Rest now," said señora Clemencia. "I have sent a telegram. Someone will come for you soon." Señora Clemencia helped Pepe crawl under the colorful quilt. She gently brushed a tear from his cheek, then kissed him and went away.

Pepe waited three days and three nights, but no one came for him. On the fourth day, the landlord unlocked the door with his key. Pepe was curled up on the bed. In his arms he cradled the last rag doll he and his grandmother had made together.

"You have to leave now," said the landlord. "I have a new family waiting to move in."

"But I have nowhere to go," said Pepe, his small body trembling with fear.

"That is not my problem," said the landlord. "I let you and your grandmother live here, even though you were behind on the rent. The furniture must stay, but you may take whatever belongings you can carry."

Pepe looked down at the quilt he had made with his grandmother. He stood up and began to fold it carefully. "Where will I go?" Pepe whispered to himself.

The landlord cleared his throat and avoided Pepe's tear-filled eyes. "Some boys live under the bridge. Perhaps you could join them."

Pepe rolled the folded up quilt and tucked it under his thin arm. Before leaving the only home he had ever known, Pepe grabbed the one other thing he could carry: his grandmother's sewing basket. Inside it he placed the last rag doll. As Pepe stepped out into the yard, the landlord reached into his pocket and pulled out a handful of coins. "Here," he said.

Pepe somberly thanked the landlord and put the coins inside the basket. Then he crossed the yard he had always swept so carefully and headed down the street.

All day long Pepe walked through town, his heart heavy and cold as stone. He passed by the beach where he and his grandmother used to sell their dolls. He went to the market and used the landlord's coins to buy something to eat. The market was as busy and loud as ever. No one except Pepe seemed to notice that his grandmother was gone.

Finally the sun began to set. The vendors packed up their unsold wares and drifted away. Pepe didn't know where to go. He saw a group of street boys hauling plastic bags filled with empty bottles. Pepe walked slowly so they wouldn't notice him, and followed the street boys home.

At the bottom of a steep, trash-strewn embankment was a miserable shantytown.

Pepe carefully picked his way down the slope and wandered through the maze of tents and boxes and rubbish. A fire was burning in a large pit underneath the concrete bridge. Several boys were roasting fish over the open flames. Smaller children counted bottles and cans. Two older boys were stick-fighting while others cheered them on. The boss boy sat by the fire, supervising everything while balancing himself on his chair's hind legs.

"Who are you?" he called out as Pepe crept closer to the fire.

"I'm Pepe."

A sound like the rustling of cane leaves swept past Pepe as his name was whispered from one boy to the next.

"What do you want with us, Pepe?"

"I…need a place to stay," said Pepe,

desperate and humble.

The boss boy looked at Pepe for a moment, sizing him up. "What can you do?"

"*Do?*" asked Pepe.

"You can't stay here for free, you know." The boss boy tipped his chair forward in order to explain. "You got to have a job—a skill—some way to contribute to our little family. I'm Primo. I make push cars out of tin cans."

A small boy rushed forward and proudly displayed one of Primo's cars. It was made from bottle caps and aluminum cans that had been cut and hammered flat.

Pepe thought for a moment. He looked down at the basket hanging from his hand. "I can sew," he said softly.

"Sew? You can make clothes?" Primo

jumped up, enthused.

Pepe looked around and noticed that all the children wore clothes that were dirty, torn, and either too large or too small. He shook his head, sorry to disappoint the boss boy. "Not for people."

Primo scoffed. "Not for people? Who else wears clothes?"

The other children laughed and waited to hear Pepe's reply. With his cheeks burning, Pepe stooped to open his grandmother's basket. He took out the little rag doll and held it up for Primo to see.

"You make clothes for dolls?" asked Primo. Some of the other boys snickered, but most of the children drew closer, hoping to get a better look at Pepe's doll.

"My grandmother and I sold these dolls

in the market, and to tourists on the beach," Pepe explained.

Primo nodded and folded his arms across his chest. He narrowed his eyes and stared at Pepe, trying to guess the value of a boy who could sew. At last he said, "Welcome to the family, Pepe!"

One of the smaller boys came up and touched Pepe's arm. "I'm Melky. You can sleep with me," he said softly. "I have a big piece of cardboard all to myself."

Melky took Pepe's hand and led him over to the lean-to where he and several other boys slept. On the muddy ground lay a flattened cardboard box.

"See?" said the boy proudly. "It's big enough for both of us!"

Pepe managed to smile, but inside his

heart was twisting with pain. How could he lay his grandmother's beautiful quilt on the filthy ground?

"I—I have to go," Pepe said suddenly, afraid his tears would slip out and shame him before Primo and the other boys.

"Go where?" asked Melky.

Pepe could not answer. He didn't have a destination. He only knew he could not stay with the street boys under the bridge.

"Think you're better than us?" taunted Primo. He puffed up his chest and clenched his fists, his chin poked out by pride. Pepe shook his head and stepped back, clutching his grandmother's sewing basket.

"N-no. I just...I mean, I—" Pepe didn't know what to say. He could hear his grandmother's voice reminding him over

and over, "*You are not a street boy. You do not drift from place to place like a weed in the sea.*"

Pepe slowly backed away from the gang of boys. His eyes fell on the smallest boy, Melky, and to him Pepe gave the last rag doll. Then he turned and fled without saying another word.

Primo spat on the ground as Pepe ran away. "He'll be back," the boss boy said with a sneer.

3.

Pepe climbed up the embankment and ran through the empty streets, almost blinded by his tears. How could this have happened to him? How could he have nowhere to go, and no one to care for him? Pepe ran until he could go no further and collapsed onto the cement curb. He buried his face in his arms and wept.

Pepe's face was so wet with tears he almost didn't feel the tongue of a stray dog licking his cheek. Pepe stopped crying and gently stroked the lonely dog. Its fur was matted but its body was warm, and Pepe took comfort in his new friend. Together they walked up into the hills, past the houses filled with light and the faint laughter of well-to-do families sitting down to dinner.

Pepe's feet led him to the home of the wealthy señora. He went around to the back of the house as he and his grandmother used to do on cleaning days. But this time, instead of knocking at the door, Pepe lingered in the shadows. The lonely dog looked up at him expectantly, but Pepe was too ashamed to ask the señora for help. He pressed himself against the stucco wall, closed his eyes, and inhaled the delicious scent of roast pork wafting out of the kitchen window.

The quick flick of a lizard's tail woke Pepe from his reverie. Pepe jumped, and the lonely dog barked at the tiny green lizard that was calmly scaling the wall.

"Sshh!" cried Pepe, afraid someone in the house might hear. He led the lonely dog into the back alley, which stank from all the overflowing trash cans. Pepe watched with envy as the lonely dog sniffed around and found something to eat in the mounds of smelly garbage.

Pepe plugged his nose and stepped closer to the dingy trashcans. He could see half a roll and some chicken bones lying on a soiled paper bag. Pepe waved the flies away, and bit his lip as his stomach groaned with hunger.

"What are you doing?"

Pepe spun around, and was surprised to see the señora's pretty daughter, Nilda, peering through the back gate.

"I—I—was just…looking for food," stammered Pepe, his cheeks burning with shame. He wished he could turn into a tiny lizard and scurry away from the girl.

"That's our garbage," said Nilda. "You won't find anything to eat in *there*."

Pepe shrugged uselessly and pinned his eyes to the ground. He could feel the girl watching him but didn't dare say another word.

"I know you!" said Nilda with sudden delight. "Your abuela used to clean our house!"

Pepe nodded mournfully, and turned away so the girl would not see his tears.

"She died, didn't she?" asked Nilda in a gentle voice.

Pepe nodded, but still could not bring himself to face the girl. Nilda put her hand on Pepe's arm.

"Wait here," she said with a sly smile and then disappeared inside the yard.

Pepe could not decide if he should run away or wait for the girl to return. Was Nilda really as kind as she seemed, or would she tell her mother he had been picking through their trash? Just as Pepe decided to leave, the back gate opened and Nilda reappeared.

"Here," she said quickly, "take this!"

Pepe grabbed hold of the small bundle but didn't have time to thank the girl before she slipped back inside the yard.

Inside a pretty cloth napkin was a ripe mango, a tortilla, and a hunk of meat. Pepe stared at the food, unable to believe his eyes. Then the smell of the pork reached his nostrils and Pepe tore into the food, tossing bits to the lonely dog.

When their meal was over, Pepe folded the pretty napkin and put it inside his grandmother's sewing basket. Then he and the dog slowly walked back to the center of town. The wide wooden doors of the church were shut tight, and the gate to the garden was locked. Pepe peered between the rails and remembered the many wonderful afternoons he had spent in the garden with his grandmother. Before more tears could fill his eyes, Pepe whistled for the dog and walked on, trailing his fingers along the black iron fence.

The lush plants inside the garden made the air fragrant and damp. When Pepe passed under the canopy of a frangipani tree, the lonely dog stopped and barked. Pepe stood still in the cool shadows, searching for the dog's shining eyes.

"What is it, girl?" he asked.

The dog blinked at Pepe, then wiggled between the iron rails and disappeared inside the garden.

Pepe gasped. Could *he* fit between the rails, too? The bars did look a bit farther apart down near the ground. Pepe glanced up and down the empty street. Then he knelt down and pushed his grandmother's sewing basket between the iron rails. Pepe took a deep breath. He put one arm through the fence, and squeezed until the rest of his body went through.

"It's a good thing I'm so skinny!" Pepe

said to the lonely dog.

They found a soft patch of grass almost smothered by shadows and soon fell asleep under the stars.

4.

The next day, Pepe woke with the rising sun and squeezed back through the rails of the fence. The little dog stayed with him for a while but then ran off to join a pack of stray dogs. Abandoned once more, Pepe wandered aimlessly through town wondering where his next meal would come from.

Before long, shopkeepers began to arrive and the streets filled with the sounds of life. The sun shone brightly overhead, and people greeted one another as they headed off to work. Pepe stood without a purpose in the middle of the busy street and felt like a thin, dark shadow instead of a real, solid boy.

"¡Ay Dios mío!"

Pepe turned and saw a small woman with silver hair precariously perched on a rickety crate. She was struggling to open the shutters covering her shop window. Pepe quickly set down his belongings and helped the woman fold back the tall planks of wood. They were both breathing heavily when the shutters were finally put away, and the old woman had to sit on the crate and catch her breath before she could thank Pepe for his help.

For just a moment, Pepe wondered if he should beg the old woman for some money so he could buy a tortilla in the market. But then Pepe turned and saw what the open shutters revealed: a shop full of dolls! Pepe's lips fell apart in awe, and he forgot all about his own hunger as his eyes devoured the beautiful muñecas.

The old woman watched Pepe closely. She noticed that his sandals fit his feet, and his clothes were rumpled but not unclean. In his thin arms he clutched a hand-made quilt and a sewing basket much like her own. *He cannot be a street boy*, she thought to herself.

The old woman had been tricked before by boys who seemed innocent but then stole whatever they could once her back was turned. This boy did not look like a thief, but how could she know for sure? At last she stood and said, "Let's go inside and cool off. It is hot already and the day has just begun."

Pepe gave a silent nod and followed the old woman inside. It was dim and quiet in the shop, and Pepe felt the same way he used to feel when entering church for Sunday mass. The dolls were so beautiful, yet Pepe dared not touch anything for fear of leaving a smudge with his unwashed hands.

"Did you *make* all these dolls?" Pepe asked, amazed.

"Of course!" replied the old woman, with just a trace of laughter in her voice. "Muñecas do not fall from the sky!"

Pepe felt foolish for asking, but the dolls were so life-like they did seem magical. The old woman continued to watch him as he gazed in wonder at the shelves filled with dolls of different shades and sizes. Finally she asked, "Where do you live, m'ijo?"

Pepe hugged his grandmother's quilt to smother the rumbling in his hollow belly. He looked at his feet and decided to say nothing rather than tell a lie.

"Perhaps you need some water to wet your throat," the old woman suggested. She went into the back and returned with two glasses of water. Pepe was very thirsty, but drank his water slowly so he wouldn't have to answer the señora's question.

Suddenly the silence between them was filled with loud knocking on the front window. Pepe and the señora looked out at the street to see who was pounding on the glass. A short, round man with a moustache lifted his hat off his bald head and nodded at the señora. She smiled and waved in return, but then groaned as the man headed toward the door and let himself into the shop.

"Buenos días, Señora Beatriz!" The man with the moustache smiled at the señora, but something in his eyes made him look not quite happy to see her.

"Buenos días, Señor Raul. What brings you to my humble shop so early in the day?"

"Just a friendly visit," he answered in a not-so-friendly voice. "I thought you might need help with your shutters."

"I can manage the affairs of my shop perfectly well on my own, Señor Raul. I have opened and closed my shop by myself for more than thirty years!"

Pepe could tell by the way the señora pursed her lips that she didn't care for this visitor.

"Who is this?" asked the man. Pepe

realized Señor Raul was pointing at him, and looked at his feet once more.

Señora Beatriz glanced at Pepe. "This is…my helper," she said defiantly.

"Ah, so you have found an apprentice at last! What a relief. I worry about you, cooped up alone in this stuffy shop."

Again the man smiled in a way that was not quite nice, and Pepe noticed that the señora's cheeks were turning red.

"We have much work to do today, Señor Raul, so if you don't mind—"

"Yes, yes, I am very busy as well," the man replied arrogantly. "I must go to the factory and check on my workers. They depend on me so! I am like a father to them," he said with a sigh. "But that is what it means to be *el patrón*."

He turned his hard eyes on Pepe for a moment, then tipped his hat at the señora and exited the store.

"Imbécil!" The señora practically spat the word at the floor. "The nerve! Coming here to brag about his precious workers!"

"What does he make at the factory?" Pepe dared to ask.

The señora threw up her hands and exclaimed, "Dolls!" Then she looked at Pepe and started to laugh.

Pepe smiled, too, but secretly he wondered if the señora really thought of him as her "helper."

The señora pulled out a stool from behind the counter and sat down with a sigh. "Señor Raul says I am too old to run this shop on my own. But what he really wants is to get rid of me and my darlings," she said with a sweep of her arm.

"He makes cheap, ugly dolls in his factory. But people prefer to buy my handmade dolls—each one special in its own way."

"Your dolls are beautiful," Pepe said.

The señora beamed with pride as she looked around the small shop. "Yes, they bring joy to many children. But it takes so much time to make just one." Her smile faded and the señora sighed. "And my eyes are not so good anymore."

Pepe swallowed hard. "I have good eyes," he said quietly.

"We shall see," said Señora Beatriz as she eased herself off the stool. "I have some ribbon that needs cutting, and some seed pearls to sew onto a bodice. Do you think you can help me with that?"

Pepe exclaimed, "Oh, yes, Señora Beatriz!" He had never seen seed pearls or a bodice before, but Pepe would do anything to prove he was worthy of the job. "My name is Pepe," he added shyly.

The señora looked at him. She liked this boy's manners and hoped she wasn't making a mistake by taking him in. He certainly didn't *seem* like a street boy but only time would tell.

"Where did you get that sewing basket, Pepe?"

"It belonged to my abuela," said Pepe. "She taught me how to sew when I was just a little boy."

The señora tried not to smile. "Then you must have been sewing for a very long time!"

Pepe nodded and held out the quilt he had made with his grandmother. "I helped Abuela to make this."

The señora put on her spectacles, inspected the straight stitches, and gave an approving nod. Without the quilt to cover his stomach, Pepe could no longer hide his hunger. The señora heard the loud rumbling and handed Pepe the bag containing her lunch.

"Eat," she insisted. "You won't be much help to me if you faint from hunger."

"But this is your lunch," Pepe protested.

"It is not even nine o'clock," said the señora. "We will worry about lunch when noontime comes. Now eat!"

As Pepe ate, the señora set out spools

of thread, ribbon, and lace, and a box filled with tiny white beads. Then she brought out a filmy white dress fit for a tiny bride. Pepe brought in the wooden crate and the señora began teaching her new helper how to make clothes for dolls.

5.

The clock on the wall ticked loudly as Pepe sat with the señora, their needles slipping silently in and out of the fancy fabric. Pepe did his best to concentrate on his task, and didn't fidget even when his back grew stiff. He hoped Señora Beatriz would be so impressed with his work that she would hire him to work in her shop. Twice the bell rang and a customer came in to buy a doll. Señora Beatriz rose and tended to the customers, but Pepe stayed focused on his work.

When noontime finally arrived, the señora looked up at the clock, then removed her spectacles and rubbed her tired eyes. "I think we should take a break, Pepe. Can you go to the market and buy us some lunch?"

Pepe nodded eagerly and jabbed his needle into the pincushion so he could find it easily later on. Señora Beatriz opened her pocketbook and took out some coins. She gave Pepe a sharp look before handing over the money. "Two pasteles, one for you and one for me. Can I trust you to come straight back to the shop?"

"Oh, yes, Señora!" Pepe said earnestly.

She told him which vendor to buy from, and then the señora sent Pepe out into the street.

How different everything looked now

that he had a purpose all his own! Pepe was so thrilled to have earned the trust of the señora that he didn't even notice the small street boy who seemed to be following him. All Pepe wanted was to buy the pasteles and return to the shop as quickly as possible.

He was on his way back to the store with the señora's change in his pocket when Pepe felt a hand tugging at his arm. He turned and saw Melky, the littlest boy from the miserable camp under the bridge.

"Time for lunch?" he asked innocently.

Pepe looked into Melky's eyes and saw the same hunger he had felt last night before Nilda shared her dinner with him. Pepe glanced at the paper bag holding the two warm pasteles. The spare change weighed heavily in his pocket. Neither the food nor

49

the money was his to share. Pepe didn't know what to do.

"Ye—es. The señora sent me to the market, but I have to return right away. She's waiting for me."

Pepe turned away and began walking quickly in the direction of the shop. Melky trotted along beside Pepe, chatting happily.

"She makes dolls in fancy dresses. I still have your doll. I named her Luz. That was my mamá's name."

Melky pulled the little rag doll from his pocket, kissed it, and then tucked it away once more. "Are you going to stay with the señora from now on?"

Pepe shrugged and wished he could find a way to make the little boy disappear. His face was unwashed, his hair uncombed, and

his clothes were stained and tattered. What if the señora saw them together? Would she think HE was a street boy, too?

Pepe took a deep breath and stopped in the middle of the street. Melky stopped too, and glanced hopefully at the paper bag.

"If I give you some of my lunch, you have to promise to go away. You can't let the señora see you—ever!"

Melky nodded and rolled his lips together as if he could already taste the delicious pastel. Pepe broke one in half and held it out to the little boy.

"You have to promise!" Pepe insisted.

"I promise," said Melky with one hand over his heart. Pepe placed the warm pastele in Melky's other hand and then hurried back to the shop.

Inside, Señora Beatriz had cleared the worktable so that the unfinished dress wouldn't get soiled by their food. Two glasses of water and two napkins had been laid out for lunch. The señora looked relieved when Pepe came into the store.

He silently fished the change out of his pocket and set everything on the table. The señora glanced at the change and seemed satisfied. Then she opened the paper bag. Pepe's legs trembled and he fought the sudden urge to burst into tears. Would the señora send him away?

Señora Beatriz was surprised by what she saw in the bag. She gave Pepe a curious look, but her eyes were not unkind.

"Were you that hungry?" She removed the pastel Pepe had broken in half and set it on one of the napkins. Pepe looked away and said nothing. The señora sighed and removed the last pastel.

"From now on, we must make sure you have enough to eat. Whenever you are hungry, you must tell me. I am an old woman, and sometimes I forget what it is like to have a young belly!"

The señora winked and Pepe sighed with relief. They ate their lunch, and then Pepe helped to clear the table so that work on the dress could resume.

Several hours later, the delicate dress was done! Señora Beatriz carefully put it on one of her prettiest dolls and then placed the doll in the shop window.

Pepe swept the floor and wondered what would happen next. The señora seemed very pleased with his work, but it was almost time to close up the shop. Would she simply send him away?

The señora looked at Pepe over her spectacles. She could see the worry stamped on his face. "What are your plans for dinner?" she asked, knowing full well the boy had no plans.

When Pepe just shrugged, the señora sighed and said, "I guess you'd better come home with me, then."

Señora Beatriz picked up her pocketbook, took out her keys, and motioned for Pepe to follow. He quickly gathered up his quilt and sewing basket, and hoped his smile would convey just how grateful he felt. After the señora locked the door to the shop, Pepe helped her to put up the tall wooden shutters.

As they headed toward her home, a fancy car pulled up alongside them and a man rolled down his window. It was Señor Raul.

"Buenas tardes, Señora Beatriz!" he said with a greasy smile.

"Keep walking," the señora whispered to Pepe. She nodded politely at Señor Raul but quickened her pace.

"Why don't you let me drive you home?" suggested the unpleasant little man. "A woman your age should not have to walk so far after bending over a needle and thread all day long. You must be exhausted!" Señor Raul chuckled and stopped his car so the señora could get in.

Pepe watched as the señora spun on her heel and put both hands on her hips. Her eyes were blazing with anger as she spoke.

"I do not need your charity, Señor Raul. I have been making dolls since you were a boy, and I will be making dolls long after this child has become a man!"

The señora put her hand on Pepe's shoulder and he instinctively stood up straight. "Now, I suggest you go home and eat your supper. My apprentice and I prefer to walk. Good evening, Señor."

Señora Beatriz steered Pepe down a narrow side street, away from the idling car and Señor Raul's stunned face.

6.

The señora's house was not as grand as Nilda's. It was, however, much bigger than the house Pepe had lived in with his grandmother. Señora Beatriz led Pepe up the back stairs and into a room that looked very much like the back room of the doll shop. Bolts of expensive fabric were lined up against one wall, and several headless mannequins stood in the corners modeling unfinished clothes. In the center of the room was a square table covered in sewing patterns, and in the far corner stood an old sewing machine.

"The dolls I mostly keep at my shop," the señora explained, "but here at home I make clothes for my other customers— fancy clothes for weddings and other special occasions."

Pepe noticed two lovely wedding gowns that were very much like the doll's dress they had worked on earlier that day.

"Do you make clothes for men as well?" Pepe asked.

"Oh yes," said the señora and she opened a tall wardrobe that contained many fine jackets, tailored shirts, and pressed pants. The señora swept her eyes over Pepe and added, "We must make you some new clothes soon."

Pepe blushed but wondered what his

new clothes would look like. He still had the pretty cloth napkin in his sewing basket, and hoped he could turn it into something nice for Nilda—a little doll, perhaps.

"Do people come here to buy clothes, Señora Beatriz?"

"Sometimes," she replied, closing the doors of the wardrobe. "I take their measurements and then they come back a few days later when their clothes are ready."

She trailed her fingers over the old sewing machine and smiled fondly. "This has been my trusted friend for many, many years."

The señora suddenly clapped her hands, startling Pepe. "Enough! We must fill your belly before you start nibbling at the furniture! Come with me."

The señora led Pepe to a small room.

Inside was a low couch and a small table with only three legs. A stack of books took the place of the missing fourth leg.

"It isn't much," said the señora, "but sometimes I lie down in here when my eyes need a break. My own bedroom is in the front."

Pepe followed along as the señora gave him a quick tour of the house. "You have a very nice home, Señora," Pepe said when the tour ended.

Señora Beatriz smiled. "You have very nice manners, Pepe. Your grandmother raised you well. Now, go put your things in the spare room, and then come and tell me what your abuela used to make for you for dinner."

Pepe rushed into the little room and

set his grandmother's sewing basket on the table. Then he unrolled the pretty quilt, and carefully spread it out on the couch. Pepe's eyes filled with tears. He could hardly believe his good fortune. Once again he had a home and someone to care for him!

After dinner the señora showed Pepe the suit she was making for an important politician. Pepe watched closely as Señora Beatriz pressed the pedal on the floor and turned the wheel on the side of the sewing machine. Sometimes the machine would choke on the fine fabric, but the señora patiently straightened the fabric and coaxed the machine into running smoothly once more.

Pepe watched the señora and hoped one day she would teach him how to use the finicky sewing machine. But for now, he was happy to do simple tasks like sewing on buttons and lace trim.

Pepe and the señora worked late into the night. When Pepe began to nod off, Señora Beatriz sent him to bed though she stayed hunched over the fussy sewing machine. Before Pepe crawled into his little bed, he remembered to kneel first and say a prayer of thanks for the kind woman who had opened her home to him.

The next morning, Pepe woke up in the strange room and wondered if it had all been a dream. He inhaled the rich scent of strong coffee and peeked outside to see Señora Beatriz making breakfast in the kitchen. Would she really let him stay? Pepe wasn't sure, so he rolled up his grandmother's quilt and set his sewing basket by the door.

The señora came to his room with a plate of food and saw that Pepe was packing. She coughed lightly and said, "Perhaps you should leave your things here for now. No point carrying them back and forth. Now— eat!"

Pepe felt his heart leap inside his chest. He accepted the plate of eggs, and gladly did as he was told.

For the next few weeks, Pepe spent his days working with the señora at her shop. It seemed like more customers were coming in to buy dolls, and Pepe hoped that was because he was such a good helper. Señor Raul came by once more, but he left in a huff when he saw how busy they were.

In the evening, they closed up the shop

and went home for dinner. Afterward, the señora taught Pepe how to make clothes for the town's fine ladies and gentlemen.

"You're a fast learner," said the señora one evening as she rested her weary eyes. "Perhaps one day, you will become a tailor and open your own shop!"

Pepe's eyes grew large as he imagined himself running a shop as successful as the señora's. He looked around the sewing room filled with suits and gowns, and just one or two pretty dolls.

"Actually," confessed Pepe, "I think I would rather become a dollmaker like you."

The señora was touched, but her smile was a little bit sad. "In the future, people may only want to buy factory dolls. They are cheaper, and easier to replace." She sighed and put her spectacles on so she could get back to work.

Pepe thought of Señor Raul who only cared about money and telling his workers what to do. "I think people will always want to have something beautiful that was made by hand. Your dolls are one of a kind!" Pepe insisted.

"Perhaps you are right," admitted the señora. "But Señor Raul's factory workers can make one hundred dolls in a day, and the poor cannot afford our lovely muñecas."

That night as he lay in bed, Pepe thought about what the señora had said. It was true that only people of means could afford the clothes and dolls they made. Pepe thought of the little rag dolls he used to make with his abuela.

"When I have my own shop," Pepe whispered to the moon, "I will make beautiful muñecas that everyone can enjoy."

7.

One evening on their way home from the shop, Señora Beatriz told Pepe she had to go out of town. Pepe's heart crept up into his throat. Would the señora send him away? If she did, where would he go?

"I need you to stay here and finish hemming those trousers," said the señora. "I will return tomorrow morning. If Señora Rodriguez didn't live so far away, I wouldn't have to stay the night."

She stopped and looked at Pepe, who was blinking back the tears of panic that had sprung into his eyes. "Will you be alright in the house alone? It's only for one night."

Pepe's throat was too tight for him to speak, so he nodded and tried to look brave. The señora was only going away for one night! He wasn't going to be homeless again.

"Señora Rodriguez has a daughter who's getting married. My mother used to work as a cook in their home. They could easily afford to buy a gown in a fancy store, but Señora Rodriguez insists I make it myself."

The señora sighed and looked down at her stiff fingers. "At least she's sending their driver to fetch me so I won't have to take the bus." The señora put her hand on Pepe's shoulder and leaned on him a little as they walked the rest of the way home.

As soon as the señora pulled away in

the Rodriguez's car, Pepe sat down and began working on the trousers that needed to be hemmed. With nothing to distract him, Pepe finished his task before too long. He carefully hung the trousers inside the wardrobe and looked around for something else to do.

Pepe's eyes fell on the sewing machine. Señora Beatriz had been working on a gown for another bride-to-be. Pepe wandered over to take a closer look. If the stitching wasn't too complicated, maybe he could help the señora by finishing it himself!

Pepe knew the sewing machine was temperamental. He knew it could run along just fine for a while, and then suddenly chew up the expensive fabric. Señora Beatriz had a way of calming the machine whenever it threw a fit. Pepe had seen her do it a dozen times. He was sure he could do the same thing himself.

Pepe worked on the gown for nearly half an hour before the sewing machine started to fuss. Pepe did all the things he had seen the señora do whenever the machine seized up. The needle refused to go up or down, but Pepe knew if he kept turning the wheel the jammed needle would simply snap in half. Sometimes, when the machine was especially finicky, Señora Beatriz opened a small door and tinkered with the parts inside. Pepe decided to give that a try. He saw a small part that looked like it was bent. Pepe tried to press it flat again, and the part snapped off in his hand!

"Oh, no!" cried Pepe. "What have I

done?"

Pepe tried to fit the part back inside the machine, but the jagged little piece wouldn't stay where it belonged. Could he glue it back together? Pepe searched the entire house but couldn't find any glue. He had a few coins the señora had given him, but all the stores were closed for the day. He would have to wait until the morning. But what if the señora returned first and discovered he had broken her beloved sewing machine? Pepe just *knew* the señora would turn him out into the street.

"What should I do?" Pepe asked himself over and over as he paced back and forth. Finally he sat down in front of the sewing machine and hung his head in despair. Pepe was certain the señora would ask him to leave, and then he would have no choice but to join the other street boys living under the bridge.

Suddenly, Pepe had an idea! He snatched the broken part off the sewing machine and dashed out of the house. Pepe went straight to the shantytown where all the street boys lived. He carefully climbed down the steep slope and made his way over to the fire that burned every night.

Primo sat surrounded by a group of younger boys who were listening closely to the story the boss boy was spinning. "And that's all it took," said Primo with pride. Then he set something down on the ground. "Look at it go—it's good as new!"

The younger boys started to oooh and aaah. Pepe took a deep breath to steady his nerves and called out, "Primo!" But no one heard.

Pepe pushed his way closer to the boss boy and finally saw what the children were so excited about: a wind-up car was driving in circles on the ground.

Primo continued his story. "I found it in the trash and fixed it myself—it just needs a coat of paint."

Pepe watched the toy car and found the courage to try again. This time he practically shouted. "PRIMO!"

All the boys turned to see who dared to interrupt the boss boy's story. Primo narrowed his eyes and spat on the ground.

"Well, well, well. If it ain't Señor Pepe. I told you he'd be back!" Primo scoffed and some of the bigger boys laughed.

Pepe opened his mouth to speak but none of his words came out. Squeezed tight within his fist, the small metal part bit into his palm. Pepe opened his hand and took a step toward the boss boy. "I—I need your help, Primo."

The flames jumped and crackled, casting shadows across Primo's face. "Why should I help you?" he asked.

Pepe looked down at the twisted piece of metal. "I have a friend…who has been kind to me, and I want to fix her sewing machine to repay my debt."

"A sewing machine? What's that got to do with me?"

Some of the other boys snickered, but Primo didn't laugh or sneer. His eyes caught sight of the piece of metal in Pepe's hand.

Primo righted his chair and leaned forward.

"You know more than anyone about fixing things made of metal," said Pepe. "I thought perhaps you could help me fix the piece that broke off."

The other boys looked at Primo to see how he would react. His dark eyes were fixed on the scrap of metal in Pepe's hand.

For a moment no one spoke. Then Primo said, "Bring it here."

Pepe rushed forward and offered the broken part to Primo. The older boy picked it up, turned it over, and held it up before the fire. "What did it look like before it broke off?"

Pepe tried his best to describe the part, but Primo just shook his head. "I'll have to see the whole machine."

Primo stood and the other boys stepped back so he could pass by. "Let's go," said Primo, the metal part now clenched tightly in *his* fist.

Pepe's mouth fell open. "Go?"

Primo came around the fire and stood before Pepe. "I have to see the machine," he explained in a voice that was gruff but not unkind.

Pepe looked at the other boys ringed around the fire. What if they followed him to the senora's house? Pepe looked up into Primo's dirt-smeared face. Could he trust a boy who stole every day just to survive?

Suddenly little Melky piped up. "I know where the house is, Primo. I can take you there."

Primo glanced down at the small boy

and playfully tousled his hair. "Alright, kid. You lead and I'll follow."

Melky grinned and skipped off, proud to help his hero. Primo began to walk away, then turned and looked at Pepe. "You coming, or what?"

Pepe knew he had no choice. He had to trust Primo. Pepe nodded and hurried to catch up with the other boys.

8.

When they reached the señora's house, Pepe stopped in front of the gate. "Please— you must promise me that you won't touch anything!"

"What?" Primo frowned and tried to push Pepe out of the way, but Pepe wouldn't budge.

"Please," he pleaded. "The señora's house is full of...special things."

"What kind of special things?" asked Primo.

Pepe looked at Melky whose eyes gleamed

with their shared secret. "The señora makes dolls!" Melky finally blurted out.

Pepe sighed, knowing this was a chance he had to take. "Come inside."

Pepe led the two boys up the back stairs and into the señora's sewing room. As soon as the light was switched on, Pepe heard the boys gasp in wonder. Melky danced around the room, brimming with delight. Primo stood frozen in the center of the room, his mouth open wide with awe.

"Please," begged Pepe, "don't tell the other boys."

Primo closed his mouth, dimmed the wonder in his eyes, and turned to Pepe. "Where's the machine?" he asked in a gruff voice.

Pepe led him over to the table where the

senora's sewing machine sat idle.

"Show me where the part's supposed to go," ordered Primo.

While the older boys examined the broken machine, Melky sat on a bench and carried on an imaginary conversation with one of the life-size dolls. Every so often he would call out to Pepe, "I'm not touching anything!" But it was hard to keep his fingers to himself.

Finally, Primo figured out how the part fit inside the machine. Pepe gave him paper and a pencil, and Primo drew a picture of what the part ought to look like. He put the drawing and the broken part into his pocket.

"You got anything to eat?"

Pepe hesitated. "Tortillas and beans?"

Primo nodded, and Pepe glanced around

the room before heading off to the kitchen. He hoped he would notice if anything was missing when he returned.

Primo walked over to the bolts of cloth that were propped against the wall. He glanced over his shoulder, then rubbed his fingers on his pants and touched the satiny white fabric. Melky, seeing his hero breaking the rules, took a lace veil off one of the mannequins and set it on top of his own head!

When Pepe came back carrying a plate of food for his guests, both boys were posing in front of the mirror. Primo had a piece of raw silk wrapped around his slender body. Melky held a bouquet of dried flowers in his hands, the veil trailing down his back like a mane.

Pepe opened his mouth to protest, but then he remembered how *he* had felt when he first discovered the señora's sewing room. Pepe set the food down on the table and went over to the two boys.

"You're wearing it wrong," he told Melky before straightening the tiara and settling the veil around the boy's narrow shoulders. Melky looked at his reflection in the mirror and beamed like a bride.

Primo carefully replaced the piece of silk he'd been wearing. He didn't look at Pepe, but softly murmured, "Sorry."

Pepe went over to the wardrobe and took out a finished jacket. "Try this," he said, passing it to Primo.

The older boy flushed, then reached out a trembling hand. Primo didn't put the jacket on right away. Instead he traced all the seams and gently fingered the shiny brass buttons.

"I stitched that one myself," Pepe said with pride.

"You made this?" Primo asked, amazed.

"I helped," said Pepe. "The señora showed me how to cut out the pieces, and then she let me stitch some of the seams on her machine."

This time Melky was impressed. "You can sew!"

Pepe glanced at the broken machine. "Well..."

Primo grinned. "*You* broke it, didn't you?"

Pepe nodded bashfully. Then all three boys started to laugh!

Pepe grabbed the jacket and held it up so Primo could try it on. Then he snatched a blue satin cape off the rack and strutted around the room like a matador. Melky began to charge at Pepe like a bull. Primo found a piece of red satin and joined in the fun!

After a while the boys grew tired and stopped their game to eat the food Pepe had prepared.

"Do you really live here?" Melky asked enviously.

Pepe nodded and showed the boys where he slept at night. "Señora Beatriz has been very good to me."

Pepe turned to Primo. "Do you really think you can fix her sewing machine?"

Primo carefully took off the fine jacket

and hung it inside the wardrobe. "I will try," he told Pepe. "But first I must go get my tools."

"I'll get them!" cried Melky. The small boy dashed for the door and was halfway down the stairs before he realized he was still wearing the tiara and veil!

The boys worked late into the night. Melky tried to stay up and keep the older boys company, but eventually he fell asleep against one of the large dolls. Pepe carried the small boy into his room and laid him on the bed. Then he rubbed his eyes, and went into the kitchen to make some coffee.

Primo was tired, but determined. He used his tools and scraps of metal to make three different replacement parts. The first was crushed by the wheels that turned inside the sewing machine. The second was spat out and flew across the room, lodging in the wall. But the third part fit perfectly! Pepe turned the crank and pressed the pedal, and the sewing machine hummed happily.

"You did it! You fixed the señora's machine!"

Pepe wanted to hug Primo, but instead he extended his hand. Primo shook it heartily and grinned.

"I knew I could do it," he said to himself. "I knew I could!"

It was almost dawn. The boys finished their coffee and talked quietly about their hopes for the future.

"You could be a tailor," said Primo. "If I were rich, I would hire you to make all my clothes!"

Pepe smiled and wondered if he could tell Primo the truth. Here, in the señora's sewing room, the boss boy didn't seem so tough. In a soft voice Pepe said, "I want to be a dollmaker when I grow up."

Primo blinked but didn't say anything at first. Then his eyes lit up and he whispered excitedly, "There are dolls that talk, you know!"

Pepe was too amazed to speak, and so Primo rushed on. "I saw one in a store once—the doll had eyes that opened and closed, and it could say, 'Mamá'!" Primo looked down at his hands. "I bet I could make a doll that talked—maybe even a doll that walked!"

Pepe nodded enthusiastically. "I'm sure you could! You fixed that wind-up car, and the señora's sewing machine. Maybe we could have our own factory like Señor Raul. But we won't be mean to our workers. And we won't make cheap, ugly dolls!"

Primo smiled but his eyes were dark and serious. "If I ever own a factory, I will ask all the street boys to come and work for me. And I will build a house with enough beds for everyone."

"Then no one would ever have to sleep under the bridge again," said Pepe quietly.

Primo and Pepe found they had much to discuss but before long, they both fell asleep with their heads resting on the table. The boys were sleeping so soundly they didn't hear Señora Beatriz coming up the back stairs.

9.

"Pepe?"

The señora stood in the doorway surveying her sewing room with wary eyes.

Primo woke first, saw the señora, and jumped up from the table. He called to Melky to get up right away.

Pepe stirred slowly. His neck was stiff from falling asleep at the table. When his eyes finally fell on Señora Beatriz, Pepe scrambled to his feet.

"Señora, you're back!"

"Yes, Pepe, I have returned," she said

with a frown.

Just then Melky stumbled into the room, rubbing at the sleep in his eyes. "Is it time for breakfast?" he asked with a yawn.

Primo yanked Melky's arm and tried to pull him over to the door, but the Señora was blocking the way.

Pepe's heart fluttered in his chest. He could tell Señora Beatriz was displeased. "Señora, these are my friends, Melky and Primo."

The señora's eyes swept over the two street boys. She did not bother to hide her disdain at their filthy clothes.

"Thought you'd have a little party while I was away?" asked the señora in a stern voice.

"Oh, no, Señora! I would never do that!"

cried Pepe.

Primo put his hand on Melky's shoulder and pushed him toward the door. Señora Beatriz held up her hand.

"Not so fast, you two. Pepe, I demand that you tell me what has been going on here!"

Pepe tried hard not to cry. He knew he had disappointed the señora, but he desperately hoped she would forgive him once he told her the truth. Pepe took a deep breath and began.

"After you left, I hemmed the trousers just like you said, Señora. But then I wanted to do more and so I—I began working on the wedding gown you left at your sewing machine." Pepe dropped his eyes, ashamed.

"You used my machine?" asked Señora

Beatriz.

"Yes, Señora, and…I'm so sorry, but…I broke it!"

The señora's eyes flashed with anger. Pepe rushed to finish his story. "But Primo is good at fixing things, and so I brought him here and he fixed your sewing machine, Señora. Really, it's as good as new!"

The señora frowned and turned to Primo. "Is this true?"

Primo shrugged and stared at the floor. "Try it and see," he mumbled nervously.

Señora Beatriz sat down at her machine and put a scrap of fabric under the needle. She carefully began turning the wheel and watched with amazement as the machine hummed along happily.

The señora turned to Pepe and said,

"Hand me that dress."

The wedding gown was closest to Melky, so he carefully handed it to the señora instead. She looked into the little boy's face and said, "Gracias, niño."

Then Señora Beatriz fed the fine gown into the machine and finished the seam that Pepe had started the night before. To her surprise, the sewing machine didn't stutter or jam. Instead, it ran perfectly!

"My machine has not run this well for many years," said Señora Beatriz.

Primo still didn't dare look up. Instead he smiled proudly at the ground.

"How much do I owe you?" asked the señora.

Primo shook his head and finally looked at Señora Beatriz. "You owe me nothing, señora," he said humbly. "I fixed your sewing machine as a favor to my friend." Primo glanced at Pepe and both boys smiled shyly.

"Well, Pepe," said the señora as she stood up from the machine. "Have your friends had breakfast yet?"

"No, señora," said Pepe.

"Then we had better feed our guests! Go wash up," instructed Señora Beatriz as she headed into the kitchen.

Pepe beamed and took the other boys outside.

"I'm glad the señora wasn't mad at us," said Melky as he splashed water on his face.

"Me, too!" replied Pepe. "I was afraid she might throw all of us out into the street!"

"The señora is a kind woman," said Primo solemnly. The two other boys nodded in agreement, and then they went back inside.

Before long, a hot, tasty breakfast was on the table. It had been ages since Primo and Melky had such a delicious meal, and they ate every last crumb on their plates. Afterward, while Pepe washed the dishes, Señora Beatriz measured Primo and Melky for some new clothes.

"Can you make me a veil, too?" asked Melky.

Primo lightly slapped the back of Melky's head, but the señora only laughed.

"Are you planning to get married, niño?" asked Señora Beatriz. Melky shook his head. "Then I think, for now, a pair of pants and a shirt would be more practical."

"Can I pick the colors?" Melky asked.

Primo was about to slap him again when

the señora surprised both boys by leading them over to the wall of fabric. She moved the bolts of silk and satin aside and took out several bolts of soft cotton. "Do you like any of these?"

After Primo and Melky had picked out their fabric, Pepe helped the señora to make new clothes for his new friends. Melky played with his favorite doll while he was waiting, but Primo looked around for something else to do. Finally he went into Pepe's room and took a closer look at the three-legged table.

Primo stood in the doorway and cleared his throat. "Señora?" The hum of the sewing machine was too loud, and Primo had to try again. "Señora?"

This time Señora Beatriz looked up at him. "Yes, Primo?"

Primo coughed a little to clear his throat. "I can fix your table—if you like."

The señora's eyebrows went up. "Can you? The leg that broke off is in the shed out back. There should be a hammer in there, too."

"I have my own tools," said Primo before hurrying outside. The señora and Pepe went back to their sewing, Melky kept on talking to the life-sized doll, and Primo came back inside ready to fix the broken table.

For a while the house was filled with noise: the steady hum of the sewing machine, the loud bang of Primo's hammer, and, of course, Melky's endless chattering. The señora smiled as she glanced around the room, which had never been so full before.

"We make a good team," Señora Beatriz

thought to herself.

10.

For a long time, Señor Pepe said nothing, keeping his eyes focused on the dress taking shape in his hands. Even though he hadn't moved an inch, the old man seemed far away. Max squirmed uncomfortably. He had to know what happened next.

Finally Max cleared his throat to get Señor Pepe's attention. "So, what happened? Did Señora Beatriz adopt all of you?"

Señor Pepe did not look up. In a quiet voice he said, "You could say that."

Max waited for Señor Pepe to go on,

but the old man seemed as though he had nothing more to say. Outside, an ambulance raced past the shop and the blaring siren seemed to revive Señor Pepe.

"What can I tell you, Max? Words cannot describe how happy those days were for me. For almost a year, we were a family."

"So Primo and Melky got to stay?"

Señor Pepe nodded. "The next day, Señora Beatriz bought a small cot to go in my room. That's where Melky slept."

"And Primo?" Max had to admit that Primo was his favorite.

"Primo wanted to build his own bed, so the señora bought him some wood and she and I stitched him a mattress while Primo sawed and hammered away. He could build anything! The shed out back became Primo's first workshop. He slept out there, though many nights he stayed up late, tinkering with things. It was Primo who suggested we put jewelry on the dolls."

"What about Melky?" Max asked. "Did the señora teach him how to make muñecas?"

Señor Pepe shook his head. "Señora Beatriz sent Melky to school, but he also helped to clean up the shop once his classes were over. And in the evening, Melky taught me and Primo everything he had learned at school. He went on to attend university in the capital, and he teaches there today."

"Little Melky's a professor?" said Max, amazed.

Señor Pepe smiled with pride. "Sí, little Melky is a big man now! But inside he is still the same little boy."

"What about Primo—what happened to him?" asked Max.

"Primo was true to his word. When he grew up, he opened a factory and taught many of the street boys how to build mechanical toys. He owns three factories now. And he helped build an orphanage, too. Before she died, Señora Beatriz donated her life savings to the new home for boys."

Max was delighted. "So no one has to sleep under the bridge any more!"

Señor Pepe sighed heavily. In a sad, solemn voice he said, "I wish that were true, Max. But even today there are many children whose only home is the street."

Disappointed, Max slumped down in his seat. He looked at Señor Pepe. "Are you glad you came to New York?"

Señor Pepe blinked very quickly but did not look at Max. "When my Tío Carlos came for me, I felt my heart break in two. I did not want to go to America, and I cried every night when I first came to Nueva York. My uncle was a stern man, and I missed my friends in Honduras terribly. When I went to school, the other children made fun of me. It was a very difficult time."

Max frowned. "Did the kids at school tease you because you made dolls?"

"No, no," said Señor Pepe. "They teased me because I couldn't speak English. And then, as soon as I did learn English, my uncle took me out of school and got me a job."

"Making dolls?" asked Max.

Señor Pepe gave a sharp, sudden laugh. "¡Ojalá! My uncle became furious if I even *looked* at a doll. He said it was his job to make a man out of me."

Max had heard other grown-ups say that before. "What does that mean?" he asked Señor Pepe.

"For my uncle, it meant I could no longer think or act like a child. I had to be tough, and not be treated with tenderness as I had been by Señora Beatriz."

Señor Pepe sighed. "I learned to hide my feelings from him, and I kept my dreams to myself. He made deliveries and I went with him on his route, lifting heavy boxes on and off the truck. I pretended to be the macho boy he wanted me to be."

Max looked around the shop filled with beautiful, delicate things and tried to imagine Señor Pepe keeping all his hopes and dreams locked away in his heart.

"Did your uncle change his mind? He must have since you *did* become a dollmaker after all," Max concluded.

Señor Pepe chuckled softly and finally set aside the dress he'd been working on. "My uncle fell in love and got engaged to a wonderful woman," he told Max.

"Maria would come by our tiny apartment sometimes, and she would tidy up and cook us the most delicious meals. Around her, I could be myself. I didn't have to pretend to be someone else."

"One day Maria brought over a magazine filled with pictures of bridal gowns. She showed me the dress she wanted to wear for her wedding." Señor Pepe smiled fondly at the memory. "I told her I would make it for her as a wedding present."

Max leaned forward eagerly. "What did she say?"

"At first, she did not believe me. I couldn't blame her—I had been acting like a different person ever since I arrived in New York. But then I told her about Señora Beatriz and the doll shop back home. I told her I knew how to make fancy clothes for dolls and for adults, too."

"Then did she believe you?" asked Max.

"She wanted to, but I knew she needed proof. So I went to the garment district where my uncle and I often made deliveries. I bought a yard of white silk and everything I needed to make the most beautiful muñeca. I made the exact dress she wanted. Then I dressed the doll in the wedding gown and gave it to Maria."

"I bet she liked it," said Max.

Señor Pepe nodded. "Maria looked at me as if I were made of gold! She kissed me, and said she would be honored if I would make her wedding gown for her."

A grin spread across Señor Pepe's face. "And then she lit into my Uncle Carlos! 'Ay dios mio! How could you keep the boy from his true calling! He should be a fine tailor, not a delivery boy!'"

"My uncle was very upset. 'It is not proper,' he said, 'for a man to do such things!'"

Señor Pepe laughed out loud. "Maria was furious! She said, 'Carlos, my father is a cook in a restaurant. Is that not proper work for a man to do?' My poor tío didn't know what to say."

Señor Pepe chuckled once more and then grew serious. "But he was a good man. Maria helped to open his eyes, and then he saw me for who I really was and not who he wanted me to be."

Señor Pepe took up the dress and began sewing once more. "It was Tío Carlos and Tía Maria who loaned me the money I needed to open my own shop. And when I married, my beloved Esperanza came and turned my little shop into a beautiful boutique." Señor Pepe looked up at a photograph of a pretty woman that hung on the wall.

Max looked at the photo as well. "Did you have any kids?" he asked.

Señor Pepe shook his head and then nodded at all the lovely dolls. "These are our children." He sewed in silence for a few moments, then took off his glasses and rubbed his eyes.

"It's getting late, Max. You'd better head home. This old man needs to call it quits for today." Señor Pepe stood with a groan, his hand pressed into his stiff back.

Max stood as well and heaved his book bag onto his shoulder. "Maybe you should get an apprentice," Max suggested. "Someone to help you around the shop."

Señor Pepe nodded solemnly. "I could definitely use another pair of hands, and my eyesight is not what it used to be." Then he sighed. "Ah, but kids today—they do not want to make things with their hands. They only want to sit at a computer and play video games all day long."

Max frowned. "That's not true! All kids aren't like that," he insisted.

"No?" Señor Pepe asked innocently. "Do you know where I could find an apprentice?"

Max shifted from foot to foot. He looked around the boutique at all the lovely dresses and dolls. "I—I wouldn't mind learning how to sew," Max said quietly.

Señor Pepe smiled kindly and said, "If you come by tomorrow after school, I will give you your first sewing lesson."

Max beamed with joy. "Can you also teach me how to make jewelry for dolls?"

Señor Pepe nodded and walked Max over to the door. "It was Primo who taught me how to work with metal. Once he even made a pair of earrings for Señora Beatriz. Primo could make beautiful objects out of just about anything—wood, gold, or an old tin can!"

Max put his hand on the doorknob, then turned to face Señor Pepe. "You still miss him, don't you?"

"He was like a brother to me," said Señor Pepe with a mixture of sadness and pride. "But we still keep in touch. Perhaps tonight I will write Primo a letter and tell him I have found an apprentice at last!"

The bell tinkled as Max opened the door. Everyone in the street could see him, but Max didn't care. "Hasta mañana!" he said as he left the shop.

"Hasta mañana!" Señor Pepe replied before closing the door and drawing the blind.

There is no shame in making something

beautiful with your hands. Max repeated Señor Pepe's words over and over in his head as he walked home wearing a smile.

THE END

ACKNOWLEDGMENTS

I would like to thank all the people who have helped me with this story. My father rarely talked about his childhood in the Caribbean, but once he told me about the toys he used to make from recycled materials—tin cans and wire hangers. My father was never a big reader but I like to think I inherited some of his creativity. When I first saw Cozbi Cabrera's beautiful muñecas I was mesmerized, and her enchanting boutique served as the inspiration for this story. Mayra Lazara Dole was one of the first readers back in 2009, and Vilma Álvarez-Steenwerth generously shared her expertise as well. When I first posted chapters of the book on my blog, I received encouragement from bloggers, librarians, and educators. It meant a lot to know that my story resonated with them and I hope that young readers will enjoy the story, too!

ABOUT THE AUTHOR

Born in Canada, Zetta Elliott moved to the US in 1994. Her books for young readers include the award-winning picture book *Bird*, *The Boy in the Bubble*, *Room in My Heart,* and *The Phoenix on Barkley Street.* She lives in Brooklyn and likes birds, glitter, and other magical things.

Learn more at www.zettaelliott.com

CPSIA information can be obtained at www.ICGtesting.com
Printed in the USA
LVOW12s2029290116

472887LV00006B/398/P